The Way Back

The Way Back

Carrie Mac

orca soundings

ORCA BOOK PUBLISHERS

Library and Archives Canada Cataloguing in Publication

Mac, Carrie, 1975–, author
The way back / Carrie Mac.
(Orca soundings)

Issued in print and electronic formats.
ISBN 978-1-4598-0716-7 (bound).--ISBN 978-1-4598-0715-0 (pbk.).--
ISBN 978-1-4598-0717-4 (pdf).--ISBN 978-1-4598-0718-1 (epub)

I. Title. II. Series: Orca soundings
PS8625.A23W39 2014   jc813'.6   C2014-903383-4
                            C2014-903384-2

First published in the United States, 2014
Library of Congress Control Number: 2014940459

Summary: Colby is a thief and a drug user. Now she is pregnant.

MIX
Paper from
responsible sources
FSC® C016245
www.fsc.org

*Orca Book Publishers is dedicated to preserving the environment and has
printed this book on Forest Stewardship Council® certified paper.*

Orca Book Publishers gratefully acknowledges the support for its publishing
programs provided by the following agencies: the Government of Canada through
the Canada Book Fund and the Canada Council for the Arts,
and the Province of British Columbia through the BC Arts Council
and the Book Publishing Tax Credit.

Cover image by iStock

ORCA BOOK PUBLISHERS
PO Box 5626, Stn. B
Victoria, BC Canada
v8R 6s4

ORCA BOOK PUBLISHERS
PO Box 468
Custer, WA USA
98240-0468

www.orcabook.com
Printed and bound in Canada.

17 16 15 14 • 4 3 2 1

snatch

Colby couldn't even begin to count how many things she'd stolen, or what it was all worth if you added it all up. She and her best friend, Gigi, had met in fifth grade. About a week later, Gigi brought her along on one of her department-store errands. Her grandma needed a new bra, so they stole that, plus pockets full of hair clips and nail polish.

Gigi had been snatching things ever since she was four years old, alongside her brother Milo, who was two years older.

Their grandmother had taught them how. It was the family business. Gram sold the stolen goods in her pawnshop.

Gram had never been caught. Not even once. She told them that her own mother used to push her around in a stroller and stick things under her as they wandered along Robson Street way back when Gram was a baby.

Stealing came naturally to Colby. She was good at it.

A stinky old man sat down next to her on the bus. His suit was shiny at the elbows and knees, with a stain down the front that was probably dried vomit. He smelled like he'd pissed himself.

For some reason, the smell made her gag. She usually had an iron stomach for nasty whiffs, which this bus route always had plenty of. She put a hand to her mouth, willing herself not to barf. Maybe it was because she was high? Something weird in the eight ball? She wondered if Milo had got it from his usual dealer. She held out her hand and saw that it was shaking. Not good.

The old man pulled a book from a greasy, beat-up duffel bag. Colby squinted at the title. *9/11: Conspiracy & Cover-Up.*

Milo would be all over that. He'd probably ask if he could borrow the book.

The smell though—it was nasty. She tasted bile as she stood up. She inched through the crowd to get closer to a window that she could open for some fresh air.

Feeling woozy, she leaned on a pole. That's when she caught sight of the old man's wallet sticking out of his jacket pocket.

But one of Gram's rules was that you had to be in the right frame of mind.

As in, not high.

"No boozy head," Gram often said. She was fond of wagging an arthritic finger in the girls' faces when she was bossing them around. She never corrected Milo. In her eyes, he could do no wrong. Except for being gay. And she was working on that. She was going to pray away the gay, she claimed. It was only a matter of time. "No dope neither. Ya?"

"We know, Gram." Gigi rolled her eyes every time. And if Milo was around, she sent him a sharp glare. Gram had no idea that he did drugs too.

Milo and Gigi's mom was in jail at the moment for exactly that. It made sense that Gram was worried about drugs. Especially because Gigi and Colby didn't do a very good job of hiding their own drug use.

So, no stealing when high.

But the old man's wallet looked so easy to snatch.

She'd been downtown with Milo, and he'd scored an eight ball. They'd smoked it in the parking lot behind his apartment building, and then he had to go meet a "date."

Colby teetered on her feet.

It would've been better if she'd kept her seat, but oh well.

The whole bus teemed with nasty smells. Colby held onto the back of a seat. She wondered if she might faint. Either because she was high or because of the stench. Maybe both.

Either way, Colby went ahead and kind of stumbled forward, so she had a reason to put her hands on the bench beside the old man to steady herself. The perfect cover for snatching his wallet.

Seamless.

In one motion, she tucked it down the back of her pants and steadied herself upright. She couldn't help but grin.

"Excuse me. So sorry."

He placed a finger on the page, marking his spot, and smiled up at her. His left eye was milky white, his other a bright blue.

"Not to worry."

Way too easy.

Colby closed her eyes for a moment. Her high was slipping. But that was okay, because she had a wallet. And while she doubted that there'd be much money in it, she was pretty sure there'd be something. Even if it was just enough to buy a joint from Rookie on the corner.

She opened her eyes. One stop away. She leaned over the old man once more and pulled the cord.

When the bus wheezed to a stop at the curb, she pushed forward with everyone else and stepped off. She took a deep breath. It didn't provide the fresh air she'd hoped for. All she could smell was the bus exhaust and a waft of urine from the stairwell leading down to the First United Church basement.

Colby squeezed her eyes shut. Her stomach churned. She was going to throw up right there, in the middle of a crowd of little bent-over grannies heading home through Chinatown with their shopping carts full of groceries.

Someone tapped her shoulder.

Colby opened her eyes. A tall young woman stood in front of her.

"I saw that."

It took a moment for Colby to really see her. Blond hair, slender face, big sunglasses.

"What are you talking about?" Colby heard a slur in her voice.

The woman cocked her head and sighed. "I saw you take that old man's wallet."

"Not me."

"Yeah, you." The woman reached forward. Colby thought she was going to frisk her for the wallet, but it was just to steady Colby as she teetered. "Are you okay?"

"No." Colby shook her head.

"Do you need an ambulance?"

"No!" Colby pushed her away. She took a couple of steps backward. "I'm fine."

"You don't look fine."

"Well, I am." Colby swallowed back more bile. She had to get away from this woman, especially if she was going to call the cops. Colby dug in her purse and pulled out her phone. She tried to text Gigi, but her thumbs felt like giant, unwieldy sausages. She called her instead.

The gaggle of grannies was gone now, so Colby sank onto the bench.

"Come get me?" she said into the phone when Gigi answered. "I'm in front of First United."

Colby put the phone away. The woman was still standing in front of her, hands on her hips.

"The wallet?"

"I don't know what you're talking about." Colby rested her head against the wall of the bus shelter.

"You know exactly what I'm talking about."

"Nope." Colby glanced down the street. There was Gigi, strutting toward her as fast as she could in her high heels and the world's tightest jeans.

"Thank God." Colby leaned forward and put her head between her knees. She was okay for another moment. But when she lifted her head to say hi to Gigi, she tasted another swell of bile, and she threw up.

All over the young woman's white sneakers.

"Jesus!" The woman jumped back.

"I didn't steal anything," Colby warbled.

"What the hell, Colby?" Gigi took her arm. "What is wrong with you?"

"I don't know."

"What did you take?"

"A wallet!" the young woman practically shouted. "From an old man on the bus. I saw her."

"Look, you didn't see anything. Got it?" Gigi glared at the stranger with her famously fierce glower. "Not if you want to keep your day moving along nicely. You didn't see anything."

The woman squared her shoulders and seemed to grow taller.

"I know what I saw, and if you don't take it into the church and leave it with them, I will call the cops."

"Are you for real?" Gigi shook her head.

"Acutely real." The woman met Gigi's glare with her own.

Gigi flicked Colby's shoulder to get her attention. Colby moaned. Gigi waggled her fingers. "Give it."

"What?" Colby felt another wave of nausea grip her stomach.

"Give me the goddamned wallet, Colby."

Colby glanced at Gigi. Gigi rolled her eyes. Colby glanced back at the woman, who had her cell phone at the ready.

"*Now*," Gigi barked.

When Colby still didn't produce it, Gigi went fishing. She found it right away and threw it at the woman's barf-spattered feet. Then she hauled Colby onto her feet and steered her down the street.

"Thanks!" the young woman called after them. "You did the right thing."

"Whatever, bitch!" Gigi hollered back.

Gigi marched Colby back to Gram's pawnshop.

Once inside, Colby breathed a sigh of relief, but with it came all the smells of the dusty old pawnshop. Sweaty leather jackets, tinny metal, greasy used tools. Colby lurched back outside and threw up again.

not telling

It wasn't until Gram set a plate of spaghetti in front of Colby that anyone clued in. Colby took one sniff of it and nearly barfed right onto the plate.

"You're pregnant." Gram slid the spaghetti out of sight and narrowed her eyes at Colby. "I'm right. You're pregnant. I knew this was going to happen. I thought it would be Gigi. But you?

I didn't think it'd be you." Gram made a disapproving sound, a sort of sharp intake of breath. "I told you both." She wagged a finger at Gigi and Colby. "This is what happens when you have sex before marriage."

"I'm not pregnant." But even as she said the word, Colby knew Gram was right.

"You totally are." Gigi gawked at her. "You said you were late. And your period never came, did it?"

"Maybe," Colby said.

"Who?" Gigi stared at her. "You don't even have a boyfriend."

"A boyfriend isn't a requirement." Colby sat back, the smell of the spaghetti hanging heavy over the table. She put a finger under her nose, blocking her nostrils. "It's a perk."

"Or a curse." Gram had been divorced three times.

"Who did you sleep with?" Gigi folded her arms across her chest and stared at Colby. "And why didn't you tell me?"

"I don't tell you *everything*."

"Yes, you do."

Colby shrugged. "Not really."

"Who, then?"

"Just some guy."

Gram put a hand on her shoulder. "Was it rape?"

"No, no, no," Colby protested. "Nothing like that, Gram. Not at all."

"Well, then?" Gigi raised her voice. "Who the hell was it?"

"Doesn't matter."

"You hooked back up with Otto. That's it."

"No." Colby had broken up with Otto three months ago, and she was only a month late for her period, now that she thought about it. She knew exactly who the dad was. "Not Otto."

"Then *who*?"

But Colby wasn't ready to tell.

She might not ever be. She squeezed her eyes shut. She didn't want to think of any baby. And she didn't want to think of any father.

Her own father had disappeared. She hadn't heard from him since her birthday in November, when he'd left a message on her phone.

Happy birthday, Sparkle.

That was it.

He'd left a couple of months before that, after getting into a fight with his girlfriend, Sheila. He'd ended up shoving her, and she fell against a corner and cut her forehead. She called the cops, but Colby's dad took off before they showed up. Sheila had been screaming at him for hours about how he needed to get a job, and how he was a bum and a failure and a useless junkie. He'd been sitting in his chair in the living room, staring at the crossword in the paper, letting it all slide, but then he snapped. He lunged for Sheila, growling like a monster.

Gigi and Colby had heard the whole thing. They were in Colby's room, eavesdropping to figure out when would be a good time to slip out. They heard Sheila scream, then a thud. Then the front door slammed shut.

Then the sirens.

Colby hadn't seen him since.

He'd taken off a couple of times before but had always come back two or three days later, after a binge. He'd plod around with a guilty expression for a week or so, while booze reeked from his pores, and then he'd stick around for a while.

But this time, he hadn't come back.

And then Sheila had kicked Colby out, because why would she take care of "that asshole's bitchy kid"?

Which is how Colby ended up living with Gigi and Gram. Which is why she was having supper with them, and not her dad and Sheila. She didn't miss Sheila. Not at all. But she missed her dad. A lot.

If she'd ever really known her mom, she might've missed her too. She'd died when Colby was three. Her dad said it was a seizure, but Colby was pretty sure her mom had overdosed.

Forget mothers and fathers. They were useless.

Forget the baby.

She'd get rid of it.

No way was she going to be a mom. No way.

Colby reached for a piece of bread, then changed her mind.

Even that repulsed her.

She rested her hands in her lap instead.

Despite everything, she wanted her dad. Right now.

She wanted to tell him about the baby. She wanted to tell him about everything that had happened between the moment he'd slammed that door and this moment now. She wanted him to tell her what to do.

Gigi was still pestering her about who the baby's daddy was. Colby glanced up. Gigi's cheeks were pink with frustration. Her black curly hair bounced around her face as she yelled. Her hands flapped. Gigi always flapped her hands when she was excited.

"If you don't tell me who you slept with, I won't talk to you ever again. Seriously."

Colby shook her head.

"Then get the hell out of my house! We're more than best friends, Colby. We're *sisters*. How can you lie to me?"

"Not lying," Colby muttered. "Just not telling."

"Same thing."

"It's not. One is omission, the other is a falsehood."

"What?" Gigi stared at her, hands on her hips.

Gram slapped the table, just hard enough to get the girls' attention.

"Enough!" She pointed at Gigi. "Sit. Eat. Be quiet."

Gigi opened her mouth to protest but thought better of it and sat. She glowered at Colby. "You'll tell me. I know you will."

"And you." Gram placed a hand on Colby's shoulder. "You are not going anywhere. You live here. Pay no attention to Gigi. She's mad, that's all. You keep your secrets if you want. We all have them."

"Thanks, Gram. Don't tell anyone I'm pregnant, okay?" Colby caught Gigi's angry gaze. "No one. Please?"

"Just Milo."

"*No one.* I don't even know for sure. And maybe I'll have a miscarriage." No way was she going to mention abortion in Gram's company. Gram firmly believed that abortion was murder. "Please don't tell."

"We won't tell anyone. Not yet," Gram said. "If you change your mind, you tell us. Then we tell only if you want. For now, it's a secret."

"Who was it?" Gigi tried again.

"Secret," Colby murmured.

"We don't have secrets. Not between us, Colby. Come on."

"So what if she wants it to be secret?" Gram shrugged. "That's okay."

Gigi narrowed her eyes at Colby. "It was Mick, wasn't it? I bet you slept with him to get back at Otto."

For a moment, Colby debated saying it was Mick just to shut her up. But just knowing wouldn't be good enough for Gigi. She'd want details, and that's when Gigi always caught Colby in a lie.

Colby shook her head. "Not Mick."

Colby stood up. "I'm going to go lie down."

"Not in my room," Gigi said. "Traitor."

"Yes in your room," Gram said. "It's Colby's room too."

But Colby ended up in the bathroom instead, kneeling in front of the toilet. She'd never been so grateful for a clean toilet in all her life. Between bouts of barfing and dry heaves, Colby thought about the boy who was the father. And how she'd go about telling him. If she told him at all.

the fox

First of all, Colby had to get clean. If getting pregnant wasn't enough of a kick in the pants, Colby figured she should just jump off a bridge now. Even if she wasn't keeping the baby, it wasn't fair to soak it in meth.

Twenty minutes after she peed on the pregnancy-test stick and an hour after she got high, Colby walked to the nearest Ministry of Children and Family Development office and right up to the front desk.

"I need rehab."

The secretary looked up. "Good morning." She pointed to a sign on the wall. *Please take a number*.

"I'm pregnant." Colby put a hand to her stomach. "If I wait, I'll puke. On the carpet."

"Okeydokey." The secretary wrinkled her nose, but her smile was kind. "Sit for a minute. I'll see what I can do."

Colby sat, one hand in her purse on the waxed-paper bag Gram had given her before she left. It was like the ones on the airplane, tall and narrow with the little tabs that fold in. Colby glanced at it. She doubted she could get all the barf into it. It was a very small bag.

Colby surveyed the people nearby, trying to distract herself. A fat woman with three kids fighting over the one piece of chalk in the play corner. Two more toddlers wrestling with a broken yellow truck while their moms ignored them. A girl about Colby's age with an infant in her lap. The baby stared at Colby with damp eyes, one finger hooked in the corner of its mouth.

"Boy or girl?" Colby asked.

"Boy." The girl gave him a half-hearted bounce on her knee.

"What's his name?"

"Aiden."

"That's nice." And then the nausea welled up again and Colby stared at her feet, gripping the barf bag in one hand.

"You pregnant?" the girl asked.

Colby nodded.

"Congratulations." There was snark in her tone. Colby wasn't sure what to say back. "What are you going to do?"

"Do?"

"Like, get rid of it? Or have it?" The girl blinked at her. "I had, like, three abortions before I had him. And I only had him because I didn't know I was pregnant until, like, way too late. I thought I was getting fat."

Colby straightened. "Wow."

"So?"

"What?" Colby put a hand to her mouth and muttered, "Excuse me." She lurched to her feet and ran out the door. She managed to open the bag, but, as she suspected, most of the vomit splattered onto the sidewalk. She put a hand on a wall and heaved. "Stupid bag." She flung it to the ground.

An old lady waiting for the bus handed Colby a wet wipe. "There you go, dear. Take a breath. Get it all out."

"Thank you." Colby heaved again, but nothing came. "I'm pregnant."

"Oh, lovely!" The old lady handed her another wet wipe. "I love babies. I love their wee toes. And their soft heads."

"Me too," Colby blurted.

"Must be on my way. You keep these." She handed Colby the packet of wet wipes. She put her palm on Colby's flat tummy. "Congratulations, dear. What a gift."

Colby returned to the office. She didn't know if she liked baby toes or their soft heads. She'd just said it because she wasn't sure what else to say. She'd looked after kids sometimes, but never little babies. She didn't know if she liked babies at all.

The girl with the baby was gone, and Colby was glad for it. She didn't want to answer any questions about what she was going to do with the baby.

When she thought about getting rid of it, she felt a wash of anxiety flush through her.

When she thought about having it, she felt the same wash of worry.

Right now, she needed to get clean.

The secretary waved. "Ready for you."

She pointed Colby toward a door held open by a slender man wearing a blue bow tie and blue-and-green-striped suspenders.

"That's a pretty gay outfit," Colby said as he ushered her through.

"That's the point." He led them to his office, decorated with framed art of foxes. Illustrations, paintings, even the print on the curtains had jolly little foxes on them. Colby sat. "Now, what can I do for you?"

Colby pointed to the row of ceramic and plastic foxes lined up along the front of his desk. "What's with the foxes?"

"Dapper and debonair. Like me. I collect them."

"No shit. Super gay."

"No shit, indeed. I'm Mr. Horvath, Super Gay."

"You're not old enough to be called mister."

"Then you can call me sir."

"All right, *sir*." Colby picked up a small plastic fox and turned it in her hand.

"Now, let's talk about you." Mr. Horvath sat back and crossed his legs. He gripped his top knee with both hands and smiled. "Janet at the front mentioned rehab. You want to go to rehab."

"Yeah." Colby nodded. "Right away. Like, now."

"That's unlikely." Mr. Horvath uncrossed his legs and pulled his chair to his desk. He typed something and stared at the computer screen. "Typically it's a six-week wait." He scrolled down the screen. "Puts us in mid-July."

"I'm pregnant."

Without even glancing up, he typed some more. "Okay, then. That changes things." He sat back again. "Be ready tomorrow."

"Just like that?"

"Clean mommies make for healthier babies."

"Right."

"How far along are you?"

"Six weeks."

"You sound pretty sure."

"I'm positive."

"We'll arrange a dating ultrasound while you're in rehab." Mr. Horvath stood. "I'll be right back, with a cup you'll need to pee in."

"I know exactly when it happened."

"Still. We like to be sure."

"I am totally sure."

"Yes, well, I hear that a lot. Plus, we'll test for drugs. What will we find?"

"Meth. Heroin. Some other stuff too probably."

"All right. Be right back."

As soon as he left, Colby shuffled the toy foxes closer together, filling in the gap where the one in her hand had been. She tucked that one in her purse.

Mr. Horvath came back and handed her a cup with an orange lid and a little baggie with her name on it. "Pee into the cup, cup goes into the bag, bag goes into the cupboard beside the toilet. Easy peasy."

"Where am I going?"

"Down the hall, first door on your left."

"No, I mean tomorrow."

"Meadow Farm. Near Powell River. For expectant moms or moms with kids. Lovely place."

Expectant moms. It sounded so old-fashioned, like his bow tie and suspenders.

"You've been?"

"Seen the brochures. Waterfront. Nice log buildings. Indoor pool."

Reminded, he pulled open his file cabinet and held out a brochure.

"Wait." He didn't let Colby take the brochure. "All of this is based on

31

the fact that you're going through with the pregnancy. If you have plans to terminate it, we can come up with a different place for you."

Colby shook her head. She didn't want to wait six weeks for rehab, even if she wasn't going to keep the baby. She wanted to go now.

"Keeping it."

First things first. Get clean. She needed time and space to think, away from everything.

If she decided on an abortion, she'd have to leave rehab to get it done in time. If she was going to keep the baby, she wanted to do right by it. As that thought occurred to her, another one did too. If she was going to have the baby and give it away, she still wanted to do right by the baby.

No matter what she decided, getting clean was the first step.

Abortion.

Adoption.

Keep it.

Eeny, meeny, miny, moe, catch an unwanted baby by the toe.

She'd have to make a decision, but first, she'd have to make it until tomorrow without getting high.

"Thank you, Mr. Horvath."

"You're welcome. You're doing the right thing, no matter what you decide about the pregnancy. And if you decide to terminate while you're at Meadow Farm, we can make arrangements."

Colby bristled. She didn't like it when people knew what she was thinking. Gram was always doing that.

"And you can keep the fox. Consider it a talisman."

"I—" Colby didn't know what to say. And then she did. She reached out a hand, and Mr. Horvath took it, and they shook. "Thank you, Mr. Horvath. I appreciate it."

extreme barf warning

The next morning, Colby and Gigi got into a huge fight. It started while they were still in bed. Gigi had the top bunk and Colby had the bottom. Colby was just waking up, and there was Gigi's face, upside down, staring at her, her long curls trailing down.

"You have to tell me before you go."

Colby shook her head. She rolled onto her side and swallowed, already tasting the bile she knew she'd have to deal with soon.

"Tell me!" Gigi jumped down from the bunk and straddled Colby. "Tell me, tell me, tell me, tell me."

"Get off me." Colby gave Gigi a halfhearted shove. "Seriously."

But Gigi just bounced, squishing Colby's queasy stomach. "Seriously, tell me."

"Get the hell off of me or I'll projectile-puke right in your face."

"Fine." Gigi climbed off. She stood in the middle of the room, hands on her hips. "Go puke. And then come back and tell me who the hell you had sex with."

Suddenly, Colby wasn't going to make it to the bathroom. She grabbed the bucket she'd placed beside the bed and barfed.

"Nasty." Gigi grimaced. But she stood there and watched nonetheless. "Tell me."

"Screw off, Gigi."

"Screw *you*, Colby."

"Well…" Colby fought back a dry heave and smirked. "Someone did."

"That's it." Gigi shook her head. "We're done." She shoved her cell phone in Colby's face. "See this? I'm removing you from my contact list. That's right. I won't have your number. So I won't be calling or texting you while you're off at preggo-teen-mom rehab jail. And when you get back, you can find someone else to mooch off. Get out."

"Considering that my ride will be here in half an hour, that was the plan." Colby pulled off her pajamas and traded them for yoga pants and a tank top, barely one step up from pajamas. She fished under the bed for her flip-flops. "Sorry if that messes with your element of drama."

"I hate you right now." Gigi sighed. "I hope it's just the pregnant you that I hate. I hope that when you get an abortion, you'll go back to being cool." And with that, she stalked out of the room, cell phone to her ear. "I'm calling Milo and telling him what a bitch you're being."

"You do that." Colby burped, tasting bile again. "Just don't tell him that I'm pregnant."

Milo.

Gigi's older brother.

Gigi's *gay* older brother.

Gigi's gay older brother who she'd kind of had sex with six weeks ago.

Colby slipped on her flip-flops, and then she was nauseous again. She barfed into the bucket. When she looked up, Gram stood in the doorway, holding a bag of whole almonds.

"Protein. Take a handful before you get out of bed, and it will help with the morning sickness."

"Thanks, Gram." Colby took the bag and wedged it into her suitcase. "I'd be happy if it was only morning sickness." She glanced at Gram and smiled. Gram, who had no clue that this baby was actually related to her. Gram, who was still praying Milo would turn out straight. Gram, who deeply believed that he just needed to find the right girl.

Colby had always wanted to be the right girl for Milo. The one who could make him jump the fence. And even while she knew he'd never be straight, all it took was some Ecstasy and a bottle of wine and she'd managed to convince him to give it a try. Just once.

He'd laughed the whole time, and it wasn't until she turned over and suggested that he imagine she was some hot guy that he finally got off. She thought he'd pulled out.

Guess not.

He'd joked about it after, but even he didn't tell anyone about what they did. As if having sex with her somehow made him less gay. He said she'd been his experiment.

If she didn't get an abortion, she'd have to tell Milo.

Chalk that up as one more reason to get rid of the baby.

A car honked outside. Gram reached for the suitcase, but Colby gently pushed her arthritic hand away. "I've got it. Thanks, Gram."

"You're doing a good thing. No drugs. Clear mind. You'll be able to think of a plan for how you will take care of your baby."

In Gram's mind, the baby was already a full-fledged member of the family.

If she only knew how true that actually was.

"It's early, still." Colby wheeled her suitcase down the hall behind Gram. "I was looking on the Internet, and it says one in five pregnancies end up miscarrying. Don't get too attached, Gram."

"Your baby will be fine." Gram opened the door. "I know it in here." She tapped her heart.

A minivan idled at the curb. Colby squinted. The female driver had dreads and enormous sunglasses. There were three other people in the van, one in the passenger seat and one each in the rows behind.

"I love you, Gram."

"I love you too." Gram kissed her. "And that baby." She gave Colby's stomach a pat and then turned back inside.

No one came to help her with her suitcase, so Colby went ahead and lifted it into the trunk. She came around to the passenger side and knocked on the window. The girl sitting there was fat, with a buzz cut and a lip ring. Heroin was definitely not her drug of choice.

The window opened. "Yeah?"

"Hi. I'm Colby."

"Yeah?"

"I—uh, I'm going with you guys to—"

"Meadow Farm, yeah." The girl gestured behind her. "Door's unlocked."

"I get carsick."

The girl stared at her. "Got a barf bag?"

"I was hoping I could sit in the front? It's better."

"I was hoping there wouldn't be any bitches. Guess we're both disappointed, huh?"

At this point, the driver leaned over. "I'm Tori. Hi. You're Colby."

"I need to sit in the front."

"Maybe I do too." The girl stared straight ahead. "Besides, I called shotgun."

"Colby, this is Jordan. Jordan, Colby." Tori straightened. Colby glanced at the rear seats. Two women, one sprawled on each row. The one in the very back was hugely pregnant. "How about you ride in the front after the ferry?"

"She's got a stack of magazines to read," Colby said. "Obviously, she doesn't get carsick." She glanced at the magazines. *Out, Curve, Gay Life.* Before all of this, Colby would've wondered how a butch dyke could end up pregnant. Not now.

"Actually, I do get carsick." Jordan smirked. "If I'm in the back."

"Fine." Colby flung open the sliding door and glared at the woman who was taking up the whole bench. "Do you mind?"

"I do." The woman made a big production of pulling her legs up so there was just enough room for Colby and she could still be mostly lying down.

"This should be fun." Colby pulled out her earphones and plugged them into her phone as Tori steered the van back into the traffic heading west.

"Super fun!" Tori chirped.

Not five minutes later, Colby was about to puke. She leaned forward as far as she could and barfed down the side of Jordan's seat. With the second heave, some got on Jordan's sleeve and spattered the stack of magazines.

"You *bitch*!" Jordan screamed.

"Ugh." Colby belched. "Going to barf again."

"Pulling over!" Tori said. "Hold on."

"You said you had a bag, bitch!" Jordan scrubbed at her sleeve with a napkin. "It's all over me."

"Told you I'd get sick if I sat back here." Colby leaned back. She pulled a wet wipe from her bag and wiped her face with it. She took a sip of water and popped a mint into her mouth. While Tori helped Jordan clean up, Colby closed her eyes. Her head ached, her stomach rumbled, and she wanted to get high.

Meadow Farm

Once Colby was released from the medical detox wing, Meadow Farm was pretty awesome. If she didn't include the agony of her first couple of days there, she could imagine that Meadow Farm was a lot like the summer camps Colby never went to as a kid. There was a main lodge—where Colby stayed in a room with three other girls—a pool and a nightly campfire. Small cabins for moms and their kids ringed the actual meadow, and there was a playground, and a trail led down to the beach. The counselors were all mellow and easy-going, and no one asked nosy questions.

So far Colby hadn't told anyone that she was pregnant. She didn't want to talk about it, so she let people think she was already a mom. There were several girls whose kids were in foster care. She let everyone think she was one of them. She didn't lie about it. She just didn't say otherwise. The girls who were pregnant never shut up about it. It didn't matter if they were keeping the baby or not. They talked about being pregnant. A lot.

Colby didn't want to talk. Maybe not ever. And there'd be no reason to, once she had an abortion.

Or if she had an abortion.

Or once she decided to keep the baby.

Either way, it was nobody's business.

Either way, Colby couldn't decide.

She wanted the baby. She didn't want the baby.

She wanted to get high. She didn't want to get high.

She wanted to be at Meadow Farm. She didn't want to be at Meadow Farm.

She wanted to tell Milo. She didn't want to tell Milo.

Well, that last one wasn't quite true. She did want to tell him. Just not yet. Whenever they talked on the phone, she could tell that he knew there was more to what was going on. Colby was sure that Gigi hadn't told him, even after their fight. But still, he knew something was up.

And then, one night about a month into her ninety days, she woke up and knew, even while she lay in bed staring at the little toy fox she'd placed beside the alarm clock that now blinked 3:32 AM, that it was time to tell Milo. Something had shifted, and now the decision to tell him seemed like the most obvious thing in the world. She could hardly believe that she hadn't already told him. What had she been thinking?

And then she remembered all the other decisions that she hadn't made. The ones she was pushing out of her mind. Ignoring.

The only one that was easy now was not getting high.

In case she kept the baby.

For herself. Or to give away.

Too hard to think about.

Colby put the fox into her pocket and slipped past her roommates and down the hall to the lounge. There was a little room off to one side, just big enough for a couch, a side table and a lamp. The couch was heaped with pillows and had a knitted throw at one end. There was a box of Kleenex on the table, and a notepad and pen.

This was where people could go to get in touch with their family and friends. Have conversations in private. Make amends over the phone, if they were at that step in the twelve-step meetings they had around the campfire each night.

People were supposed to book the room, in half-hour chunks. Colby hadn't. But it was empty. She slipped into the room and shut the door. She opened the window and took a deep breath of the salty sea breeze. The moon was nearly full, high and glowing above the water. Colby curled up on the couch and pulled the throw over her lap. She stared at the moon.

She sat like that for a few moments, holding her cell phone in her hand.

Milo probably wasn't even home. Or if he was, he probably had a date.

Colby closed her eyes and imagined him in his bed. He lived in the West End, in a tiny loft apartment no bigger than Gram's living room.

His bed was up a set of stairs, in the loft part, which was above the kitchen. It was a new bed frame but made to look like one of those really old-fashioned wrought-iron ones. Milo had an expensive mattress that one of his boyfriends had bought for him. At least, Colby thought it was an actual boyfriend, not one of the men who just paid him for sex.

Colby squeezed her eyes tight, pushing away the image of Milo and some old guy having sex. She hated that he made money that way.

Before she lost her will, Colby brought her phone to her ear and listened as it rang. And rang. And rang.

She got his message. *"You've reached the blazing-hot saddle of Milo. Leave me your details and we can arrange for you to* come *for a good time.*"

Colby hung up.

She was just about to try him again when her phone rang.

"Where the hell is this Meadow Farm prison?" Milo yawned. "Is it awful? Do you hate it? Can I come rescue you? I'm dating this guy who has a car. Like, a nice car. That actually works. Not like that piece of crap Timothy had."

"Hi, Milo."

"Hi, Colby." Milo yawned again. "Kiss, kiss."

"Were you sleeping?" asked Colby.

"Yeah. Weird, right? Totally crashed."

"Binge?"

"Never mind," he said. Colby could hear him lighting a cigarette. He took a long pull and spoke as he exhaled. "Tell me everything about the exciting life of a teenage girl in rehab. Have you met a big ol' dyke and jumped the fence?"

"Big ol' dyke, yes. No fence jumping."

"Deets. I want to know everything."

"I have to tell you something."

"Tell me *everything*."

Colby pulled at a loose thread in the throw. She wound it around her finger.

"Are you alone?" Colby winced, not wanting to know if he wasn't.

"Absolutely."

"Are you lying?"

"No, actually." Another drag of his cigarette. "I was out until 2:00 AM, and then I kicked Topher out. My new boyfriend. Topher. His name is actually Christopher. But everyone calls him Topher. I totally had to sleep. I hadn't slept in, like, five days."

"High much?"

"Let's not talk about that. You're in rehab. Oh my god! Rehab! What the hell, Cole? What are you doing in rehab? Gram told me and I was, like, what the hell is Colby doing rehab for?

And Gram said you'd tell me in good time."

"Good time. Right."

"Good time. So spill."

"Oh, Milo." Suddenly, Colby was crying. Full-on sobbing. She grabbed a tissue and wiped her eyes. "I'm pregnant."

"Wow." A long silence. "Colby. Jesus." Milo's tone was lower now. Serious. "Really?"

"Really."

"Oh my god." Milo said the words slowly. "Who? Please tell me it's not Otto. You didn't sleep with him after you dumped him. Did you? Break-up sex is so overrated. I am so not a believer in break-up sex."

"No. Not Otto."

"Was it that guy we met at the club?" Milo laughed. "The one with the nose?"

He meant the guy who'd been grinding Colby's ass on the dance floor.

He was hot, and it was true that the guy and Colby had left together. But only as far as the bus stop, where Colby had been overcome by a wave of nausea. Which made sense now.

Besides, Colby had already told Milo all of that.

Milo knew she hadn't slept with him.

Either he was slow figuring it out, or he already had and didn't want to say it. Then he did.

"Not from that one time?"

"Yes. From that one time."

"Not me."

"Yes, Milo. You."

"No way."

"Yes way."

"No way! Otto. It has to be Otto's."

"It's not Otto's. After I dumped him, I got my period. Then you and I messed around. And now I'm pregnant."

"But I'm *gay*."

"And I'm *pregnant*."

"I can't be a dad!"

"Hang on, Milo." Colby stopped crying. She shifted from sad to mad in barely an instant. "No one's asking you to be a *dad*."

"But you're pregnant. With a baby. And you've just told me that I'm the dad."

"Consider yourself a sperm donor, if that helps. Whatever! I'm not even keeping it."

"You cannot—"

"I can so!"

"You wouldn't!"

"I totally WOULD. I've got two more weeks to decide."

The way they were arguing back and forth reminded her of when they were kids. They'd fought all the time. Usually over Gigi. Or the remote control. Both she and Milo always cared deeply about the outcome, no matter what they were fighting about. That much hadn't seemed to change.

"Cole?" Milo barely whispered. "I'm so, so, so, so sorry."

"For what? For having sex with me?" Colby was only sorry that it hadn't made Milo straight.

"We shouldn't have had sex. I know how you feel about me—"

"Shut up, Milo." Colby dropped her head into her hands. "I'm not in love with you. Not anymore."

"But you are," Milo said quietly. "And that's okay. I love you, Colby. Just not romantically."

Someone knocked on the door. When Colby didn't answer, they knocked louder, and then they started banging on the door.

"Get out! I've got it booked!" It was Jordan. Who hadn't gotten any nicer as she got more sober.

And she was not pregnant.

Or a mom.

But her mother had pulled some strings and got her in anyway.

Since barfing on her in the van, Colby had learned that Jordan was a drunk and a cutter.

"Hurry up!" Jordan bellowed. "GET OUT."

"I have to go," Colby whispered.

"What are you going to do?" Milo asked.

"I don't know." There was a long pause, during which Colby could practically hear everything that Milo was not saying out loud.

Jordan banged harder on the door. "I know it's you in there, Barfy McBarfyson. Get the hell out."

"Give me a minute, all right?" Colby kicked the door. "Milo?"

"Okay, Cole." Milo sighed. "You decide. Of course it's up to you. It's your body. But let me know. Okay?"

His kind words made Colby cry even harder. She wanted him to scream at her. She wanted him to lecture her on how wrong abortion was. She wanted him to be an asshole and demand a paternity test. She wanted him to make her decision easier. Instead, he was making it harder. Just by being nice.

"I will." Colby blew her nose. "I have to go."

"Call me later?"

More banging on the door.

"I will."

"Love you, Colby."

"But not in that way."

"No, not in that way. Sorry."

"Love you too, Milo." Colby laughed. "Totally in that way."

When Colby opened the door, Jordan's face was twisted in anger. But all Colby wanted was a hug, and Jordan was the first person she saw. She flung herself at Jordan and wrapped her arms around her. Jordan stood stiff as a board for a few moments, and then she relaxed and hugged Colby back. Then the two of them went into the little room and shut the door, and Colby told Jordan everything.

home again

While it was true that Jordan wasn't particularly the sweetest person in the world, she was ace at being a friend. When Colby finally decided to keep the baby, Jordan didn't try to talk her out of it. She just listened while Colby went on and on about how she couldn't abort something that she and Milo had made together, even if it was totally screwed up and she might be a shitty mom. Jordan just patted her back and handed her tissues and told her that she'd be an amazing mama.

Jordan took care of Colby for the rest of the time they were at Meadow Farm. The other girls joked about how Colby was Jordan's "prison wife," and their counselors were always going on about how "relations" between girls in rehab were not okay. But it wasn't like that. Jordan was more like a very protective older brother. Nothing more. She looked out for Colby. She even managed to arrange for them to leave at the same time, so they could share the van ride back.

When the van pulled up in front of Gram's house, Jordan got out too.

"I got to meet this Gigi chick," she said as she hauled her duffel bag out of the trunk.

Rehab had been good for getting Jordan clean, but she'd put on weight and was even heavier now. Her clothes were too snug, so she was wearing old sweatpants for the ride home. Colby was going to take her to Value Village the next day.

Gigi flung open the front door and ran down the stairs.

"You're home!" She grabbed Colby and spun her around. "I missed you!"

"I missed you too." Colby hugged Gigi tight for a long time. "Hey, I want you to meet Jordan."

Gigi and Jordan had talked on the phone a few times when Gigi had called Colby (after she gave up on her no-contact stubbornness), but now Gigi frowned at her.

"Hey."

"Hey."

"So, where do you live?"

"My mom lives in Burnaby." Jordan pulled out a cigarette and rolled it between her fingertips. "Not sure that I'm going to go back there though."

"You can't stay here."

"I know." Jordan retreated to the end of the yard and lit her cigarette. "I just wanted to meet you, that's all." Then she turned to the street so that the smoke wouldn't go in Colby's direction.

Gigi folded her arms and took a step back. She looked Colby up and down.

"You don't even really look pregnant."

"I totally do." Colby lifted her shirt. She was four months pregnant now. She had a belly, small and low-slung, just a swelling under her belly button.

"You just look fatter." Gigi said it loudly, for Jordan's benefit.

Jordan pretended not to hear, but Colby noticed her shoulders tense.

"Thanks, Gigi. That's a lovely thing to say."

"What am I supposed to say?"

"You look great?"

"You do, actually. All healthy and shit."

"I love you, Gigi." Colby hugged Gigi again.

"I love you too." Gigi kissed her on the cheek. "And your bastard baby."

Colby lifted her shirt again and put Gigi's hand on her belly. "I'm starting to feel it kick. Just sometimes. Or maybe it's gas. I don't know. Jordan looked it up. I'm supposed to start feeling flutters around now."

Gigi pulled her hand away. "I love you, but I don't want to feel some alien creature trying to claw its way out."

"Cool." Colby glanced at the porch. Gram stood in the doorway, a dishtowel tucked into the waistband of her nylon pants. She blew Colby a kiss. "Gram!" Colby ran up the steps and hugged her. "So good to see you!"

Even as she hugged Gram, though, Colby scanned the living room behind her.

No sign of Milo.

She hadn't seen Milo since before she'd found out that she was pregnant. Despite all the phone calls and texts, she was nervous about actually seeing him. Like it'd make the baby real in a whole new, uncomfortable way.

He'd texted her and said he would be there when she got to Gram's, but Colby wasn't surprised that he wasn't. They were going to tell Gram and Gigi that night.

That he was the dad.

But Milo was never on time. Not ever. She did wish that he'd managed to be on time just this once, because waiting was worse.

Gram insisted on Jordan staying for supper. Milo texted that he was on his way and would make it there by the time the lasagna was ready to come out of the oven. He wasn't though. He didn't get there until almost nine o'clock, just as

Jordan was getting ready to catch a bus to Burnaby. He knocked on the front door, which was when Colby realized he was not as okay about everything as he constantly claimed to be when they talked on the phone. Otherwise he would've walked right in like he always did. Was he high? He was only a week out of detox, so there was a good chance. He hadn't had three months, like Colby and Jordan. He'd had forty-eight hours and willpower.

Colby opened the door. Milo stood there with a bouquet of flowers in his hand. He handed them to her and then went down on one knee. He pulled a small velvet box from his pocket. Inside was a ring with a tiny diamond set in the middle.

"Colby." He looked up at her, not smiling. "Will you marry me?"

"Are you high?" Colby asked.

"Totally straight." He laughed. "In a manner of speaking."

"Oh, this is going to be good." Jordan rubbed her hands together. "Really good."

Colby stared at him. She had no idea what to say. What to do next.

Gigi appeared behind Colby. "What the hell are you doing, Milo?"

"Asking Colby to marry me." He shifted from one knee to the other.

Colby felt the baby flutter. "Milo—"

"Clearly, detox didn't stick. What are you on? Why the hell would you ask Colby to—" Gigi suddenly stopped talking.

"I'm not high."

"Oh. I see." Gigi's hand drifted to her mouth. She glanced at Colby, then Milo. "I get it." She nodded. "I totally get it now."

"I—" Colby swallowed. She didn't know what to say.

"We—" Milo went pale.

Gram came into the room and saw Milo on one knee. "Milo? What's going on? Why are you—"

"Never mind. It was a dumb idea." Milo snapped the box shut and stood up. But it was too late.

"Praise God!" Gram clapped her hands. "You're not a gay anymore!"

"Gram, it's not what you think."

Gram grabbed Milo's hands and brought them to her lips and kissed them. "My sweet boy. Such a big heart. You will raise the baby like it's your own. You'll be so happy together. You've always loved Colby. And she has always loved you. A perfect match!"

"It is *not* a perfect match." Gigi grabbed Gram's arm. "Milo is *gay*, Gram. Nothing has changed about that."

"But he asked Colby to marry him."

"I'm still 'a gay,' Gram." Milo spoke quietly. "Gigi's right."

"I don't understand."

Jordan guffawed from the couch. "Just spit it out, someone!"

"Milo is—" Colby started.

"I'm the—" Milo tried.

"You *screwed* him. You screwed my brother." Gigi glared at Colby. And then at Milo. "What the hell, Milo?"

"No!" Gram put her hands over her ears and fled toward the kitchen. "I don't want to hear any of this. No!" She stopped at the edge of the room. "But if you had sex with Colby, then you're not gay. Right?"

Milo shook his head. "Still gay, Gram. It was a mistake."

"Milo is still gay. He is the father of my baby. We made a big mistake." Colby felt a stab of pain at the word *mistake*, but he was right. "We're not going to get married."

"But we could. Why not?" Milo stood up. He closed the ring box. "Like, a show marriage, you know? It'd be fun."

"Pretend to be married?" Gram gasped. "No, marriage is a sacred union. I cannot listen to this!" With that, she stomped out of the room. A moment later she was slamming pots and pans around, muttering angrily to herself.

"Right." Milo laughed. "Says the woman with three ex-husbands."

"Gram's right," Colby said. "I want to actually get married someday. For real."

"Me too! Then we could just get divorced. People get divorced all the time. Come on, Colby. We could totally have fun with this. Mess with people's heads."

"Haven't you done that enough?" Gigi piped in.

"We're not getting married, Milo."

"I just want to do the right thing."

"Oh, sure." Gigi laughed. "The right thing would've been not sticking your dick where it doesn't belong."

Milo and Colby looked at each other. They grinned. Then Colby giggled, and so did Milo. And within seconds, they were laughing so hard Colby though she might pee herself.

"I just wanted to see what it's like," Milo said between giggles. "Just once."

"And you didn't think to use a condom?" Gigi crossed her arms. She was not laughing.

"We were high. And—"

"Stupid?"

"Sure." Milo laughed. "We were stupid. And high. And I just wanted to see what it's like. That's not a crime, Gigi."

"You wanted to try what for once?" Gigi sneered. "A vagina?"

"I like vaginas," Jordan announced. "Definitely worth trying."

"Shut up." Gigi pointed at Jordan. "Why is that fat, ugly dyke even here?"

"Gigi!" Colby yelped. "That is so mean. Jordan, I am so sorry."

"It's okay, Colby." Jordan stood up. "I'm okay with being a fat, ugly dyke. Better than being a skinny, nasty bitch—"

"Really?" Gigi squared her shoulders. "You want to start something in my own house?"

"And on that note, I'm out of here." Jordan headed for the door. "I'll leave you three to sort this out."

"Before I beat the crap out of you," Gigi snapped. "Good idea."

"Bye, Colby." Jordan hitched her duffel over her shoulder and gave Colby a kiss on the cheek. "I'll see you soon, hon. You'll be okay here. Right?"

"Yeah." Colby put her forehead on Jordan's chest. Jordan wrapped her arms around her and gave her a tight hug. "I'll see you tomorrow."

"Oh my god, Colby," Gigi said. "When I told you to find a fat lesbo to keep you warm in rehab, I didn't mean it for real."

"We're just friends," Colby said. "She's a really good friend."

"Like I'm not?" Gigi challenged.

Colby didn't want to answer that. She wasn't sure what she'd say. She didn't trust what she'd say.

Suddenly her mouth felt desperately dry. She wanted a tall glass of ginger ale, full of ice. And a stack of graham crackers. She wanted a dark room and a comfortable bed. She wanted sleep. She wanted her dad, who didn't even know he was going to be a grandpa. She wanted Milo to want her, but not in a fake-marriage kind of way. She wanted Gigi to stop being so awful. But at least, and thankfully, she didn't want to get high.

break-in

Okay, so Jordan and Gigi were never going to be best friends. That much was clear, but after a while, they stopped always being on the brink of beating each other up. Or on the brink of Gigi going cat-fight crazy on Jordan. Jordan said she'd never hit a girl. It was a butch dyke "rule," according to her. But a few times, Colby could see she had to really work at not breaking that rule.

Eventually, Gigi even agreed to let Jordan come along on one of their jobs. She'd been watching a house up in Kerrisdale, and she was pretty sure it didn't have an alarm system. There were no signs on the lawn, and the couple who lived there came and went quickly, like they weren't taking time to set or deactivate an alarm. They had two little kids, a nanny, two cars, a housekeeper, a gardener and, as Gigi put it, "could totally afford to share their shit."

"What if they do have an alarm?" Jordan asked when they were getting close. Her role was to park Gram's car about a block away and then pull up when Colby texted her to. There was an alley where she'd idle while the others loaded up the car.

"I've got a backup plan," Gigi said. She wasn't totally high, but she wasn't exactly not high either. She was jittery and irritable. Colby knew what that was like. The sharp edge between coming down and needing more. Colby knew Gigi was just trying to stick to Gram's clear-head rule, but she was a jonesing mess.

"Care to share it?" Jordan said.

"No, actually."

There was a long silence. Colby sighed. "Everybody, be nice." And then to Jordan, "This is Gigi's *thing*. She's really, really good at figuring out which houses don't have alarms, or which ones are between alarms, or which ones aren't working. It's almost like a sixth sense."

"Thanks, Colby." Gigi smirked. "That almost sounded like a compliment."

"It is." Colby sighed again. "I'm not mad at you. You're the one playing cold shoulder."

"Well, you have your new best friend and your little trio of recovery buddies." Gigi tapped the window. "You don't need me. I just want to get this done so I can go get high." She made a pretend pout when the three of them frowned. "Oh, am I threatening your sparkly new cleanliness? Good. Park here."

Jordan pulled over. Milo and Colby shared a look, but neither of them said anything more.

Milo touched the plastic Peter Pan figure hanging from the rearview mirror.

"Everyone touch the Peter," he said.

Jordan laughed. "That's so gay."

"It's for good luck," Milo said. "Everybody touches the Peter. You too, rookie."

Jordan flicked it, sending it into a kind of aerial dance.

"Be careful." Jordan looked at Colby when she said it.

"We will." Colby felt the baby move. She put her hand to her belly.

She knew it wasn't right to be stealing. Especially with the baby. She was pretty sure that jail would suck for a pregnant woman. But they'd never got caught before, and they weren't going to get caught now either. Colby got welfare, but it was hardly anything. She liked the extra money she got from stealing. She'd have to think of a better—and *legal*—way to make some money. Right now, though, this was it. Good idea or bad idea, she got out of the car.

The house was old and very elegant. The hedge was almost as tall as the mansion-like home itself and provided good coverage. Gigi had decided that midmorning was the best time. The nanny was out with the children, the gardener came on alternate days and this wasn't one of them, the housekeeper went out for the day on Wednesdays, the husband was at work, the wife was at yoga, and the dog was with the dog walker.

Milo chose a side door and set about picking the lock. Just as Gigi was good at picking the target, Milo was good at getting them in. What was Colby good at? Not much. She was a very capable pair of hands though. And an extra set of eyes.

Once inside, Colby headed upstairs to find the master bedroom. As much as people were cautioned to keep their valuables in a safe, or at least in an odd, unguessable place, they usually didn't. Colby had good luck finding jewelry in actual jewelry boxes on the tops of dressers or out in plain sight in walk-in closets and dressing rooms. People were kind of dense that way.

Sure enough, there was a small mirror-and-silver jewelry box sitting atop a shelf in the walk-in closet, which was bigger than her and Gigi's room at Gram's.

Colby took the whole thing. She'd have a look at what was inside later. No doubt something worthwhile, if not the box itself.

She went downstairs, the jewelry box under one arm, to find Gigi and Milo.

Milo had several reusable shopping bags over his shoulder and an armload of electronics.

"Not the kids' stuff though." Colby lifted a few things out of his arms.

"You're going soft." Gigi had a wheeled shopping cart, bulging at the seams. "Bet they send the housekeeper to the store with this thing. I can't imagine the owners being caught dead rolling it down the sidewalk behind them."

"Let's go." The baby was kicking lots, and Colby was thirsty and needed to pee. "I have to go to the bathroom."

"Get over it, Colby. You're pregnant." Milo pointed to a powder room at the end of the hall. "Use that one."

"I'll wait." Colby didn't like to do normal things in the houses they were robbing. Gigi liked to help herself to their food, and Milo had no qualms about turning on the TV or taking a piss.

"No." Colby just liked to get in and get out. She texted Jordan. "Let's go."

Milo, Gigi and Colby headed to the back gate, where Jordan was just pulling up. She popped the trunk. Colby and the others put the things inside, then got into the car.

"Want some chocolate?" Gigi offered a box of expensive chocolates. "I was totally looking for candy, but this was all I could find." Colby took one and popped it into her mouth. Milo took one too, but Jordan just shook her head as she turned onto the street.

"You okay?" Colby asked.

Jordan looked pale. "Yup. Fine."

Gigi leaned forward from the backseat and laughed. "You're scared shitless."

"No, I'm not."

"It's okay," Milo said. "It takes a while to not be."

"I'm not scared."

"It's okay if you are," Colby said. She offered Jordan the bottle of water.

"I'm not scared!" Jordan shouted.

"Right," Gigi said. "Whatever you say."

"Let's just go, okay?" The baby kicked, hard. "Heck, even the baby wants to go home."

The four of them rode the rest of the way back to the pawnshop in silence. As the chocolate melted in her mouth, Colby knew that this was the last time she'd break into someone's house. It seemed different this time. Dirtier. As if the baby and being clean set a new standard of okay, and this failed miserably. Or maybe it was Jordan, and how she nearly vibrated with unease, casting a shadow of disapproval over the whole thing. Either way, Colby was done. The money had been so important when she was spending it on getting high. But it simply wasn't worth it anymore.

sparklies

When they got back to Gram's, Colby put the jewelry box on her bed and went to the bathroom again. She always had to pee these days. The bathroom was just off the kitchen, and she could hear Milo and Gigi telling Gram how it went.

"Jordan nearly pissed herself," Gigi said with a laugh.

"Didn't," Jordan muttered.

"God, did so."

Colby closed her eyes. She put her head in her hands, elbows on her knees. She opened her eyes and saw her big belly, her pale knees, her pants and underwear bunched around her ankles. The chipped linoleum. The caulk around the tub. Gigi's pink terrycloth bathrobe hanging behind the door. The sink with the rust stain. The mirror with the crack at the bottom from Gigi throwing the hair dryer at it once when she was arguing with Gram.

Colby tried to remember what Gram and Gigi had been arguing about. Going out? A mess in the kitchen? A guy Gram didn't approve of?

That was it. Danilo. The one Gram said she could tell was evil just by the look in his eyes.

And he was. Colby had pulled Gigi out of a nasty abandoned warehouse after Danilo punched Gigi in the face.

Or was she thinking of the other guy? With the motorcycle?

Colby was tired of rescuing Gigi. She was tired of stealing. She was tired of living in the middle of so much drug use, in a neighborhood plagued by it. It wasn't good for her. Or the baby.

Her ankles were swollen.

She felt like she still had to pee, but she already had. Her bladder hurt.

The last time she was with the midwife, she'd had her pee on a stick to check for a bladder infection. It'd been borderline.

She bet she had one now.

In the kitchen, Gigi and Jordan were still arguing. Colby sighed. She couldn't sit on the toilet all day, even if hiding in the bathroom seemed more appealing than refereeing those two.

She pulled her pants up, washed her hands and opened the door.

Gram had gone back to the shop.

"You think you know me." Jordan leaned forward, both hands splayed on the table in front of her. "But you don't. So stop acting like you do."

"I totally know you." Gigi laughed. "You'd like to think that I don't, but I do. You hated every minute of it. You are so transparent. It's the only thin thing about you. I can see right through you. You were scared."

"Whatever—"

"Is what people say when they know the other person is right."

"Fuck you, Gigi."

"Is what people say when they've run out of anything else to say."

"Stop it, you guys!" Milo put his head in his hands. "Give it a rest."

"Gladly," Jordan said.

"Says the one who knows she's lost."

"Lost what?"

"The debate."

"The *debate*?" Now Jordan laughed. "You think you have any debating skills at all, Gigi? For real? You're not even smart enough to enter into a debate about what kind of nail polish to put on."

"What do you know about nail polish, dyke?"

"Uh-uh." Jordan pushed back her chair and stood up. "I'm out of here. I don't need this shit, coming from some junkie bitch."

"Jordan, stay," Colby said.

"You're picking her over me?" Gigi stood up too. She glared at Colby. "Some best friend you are."

Before Colby could answer, Jordan spoke up. "You're not acting like much of one either these days."

"Stay out of it, dyke."

"STOP IT!" Colby shouted. "All of you!"

"I wasn't doing anything," Milo muttered, head still in his hands.

"I'll go." Jordan pulled her jacket on. "Want to come with me, Colby? I'll buy you one of those whipped-cream-sugar-coffee-ice things you love."

"I don't…" Colby wanted to choose Gigi. But she didn't want to deal with Gigi's anger. And besides, Gigi was just going to go get high anyway. If Colby went with her…

Colby didn't want to think about that.

She was going to stay clean. No matter what. And part of staying clean meant staying away from drugs. Which meant staying away from Gigi. The reality of that hit Colby hard. She swallowed.

"I'll come with you, Jordan."

"I'll come too," Milo said. "If that's okay?"

"Sure," Jordan said. "My treat."

"Must be nice," Gigi said.

"Okay," Jordan said with a sigh. "I'll bite. What's nice?"

"To have money."

"I earn it."

"Like it takes effort to take it from your mommy's wallet."

"I have a job."

This clearly surprised Gigi.

"See?" Jordan shook her head. "You don't know anything about me."

"Yeah, well, I have a job too." Gigi scraped her chair back and wagged a finger between Milo and Colby. "And if these two assholes won't do their part of it, I guess that leaves me to help Gram go through everything."

Gigi stalked down the hall and disappeared into the shop, slamming the door behind her.

"You know what?" Colby rested her hands on her belly. It felt hard to catch her breath. Her head felt light.

The baby kicked, as if to let Colby know that he or she was right there.

Listening. Taking everything in. All of this. The fighting. The stealing. The dark cloud of drug use hanging just overhead, threatening to break and soak them all. "I don't want to go anywhere. I just need to go lie down."

Colby stood in the hall outside the room she shared with Gigi. For the first time since getting kicked out of her dad's house, she wanted her own room again. Her own place. Away from all of this. Away from Gigi.

But she had this room. This was it for now.

Colby sat on the bed. She rested the jewelry box in her lap.

When she opened it, she gasped.

Right on top lay a necklace encrusted with diamonds, nestled on one of those black velvet molds that keeps the necklace in the right shape.

Beside it, a small black velvet box. Inside were matching earrings.

A sapphire bracelet tucked in a velvet drawstring bag.

Four gold rings in one of the drawers. One that looked very old and had a large solitaire diamond in a delicate setting.

And a small gold bangle, meant for a child.

There was an inscription on the outside. *Guess how much I love you?*

And on the inside too. *Up to the moon and back.*

Colby felt as if someone had grabbed her heart and squeezed. She had to concentrate on taking a deep breath, and it was hard.

This bracelet didn't belong here. In Gram's house. In Colby's hand.

None of the jewelry did.

It didn't belong to them.

Colby would take it all back.

She heard Gigi coming down the hall, talking on her cell. Colby shoved everything back into the box, slammed it shut and slid it under her bed.

Gigi opened the door and saw Colby. She rolled her eyes.

"I thought you went out with your faggot fiancé and lesbian lover-best friend." Without waiting for a reply, Gigi turned on her heel. "No," she said into the phone. "Just Colby and her gigantic belly, taking up space in MY room. I'll meet you in ten minutes. Yeah, I've got money."

When she was gone, Colby opened the jewelry box again. She touched the child's bracelet.

She'd give it all back. Just drop the box on the front step and take off.

Not right away though. They'd be hypervigilant now. And besides, she had to go pee in a cup for Mr. Horvath. But first, a nap.

hey, baby

For whatever reason, no one asked about the jewelry box. Colby figured that Jordan and Gigi had been too busy hating each other to remember it. Milo probably hadn't noticed it in the first place.

Gram did ask if anyone had found any jewelry, but when they all said no—including Colby—she hadn't pushed.

Nor did anyone mention the box. So it stayed under Colby's bed, while she tried to figure out when to take it back.

Colby was enormous now. It was hard to find a comfortable position at night, and so she tossed and turned, shoving various-sized pillows under her hips, between her knees, along her back. Nothing was comfortable. She hardly slept, which left her with long dark nights to do nothing but think.

About how to move out of Gram's. About where her dad might be. About the baby. About how it would feel to be a mom.

Sometimes she'd get a sudden pain. Practice contractions, her midwife told her. They didn't mean that the baby was coming, just that her body was getting ready. At first, Colby had been terrified of them. But at night, when she was lost in a sea of dark thoughts, she appreciated them for kicking her back to reality.

If it was early morning and Colby couldn't get back to sleep, she'd get on the bus and go see Jordan at work. Jordan's new job was at a coffee shop called the Velo Café, which had a bicycle drive-through window. It was owned by one of her mom's ex-boyfriends, a hipster with a beard and thick-rimmed glasses and a wardrobe full of skinny jeans that didn't suit his tubby figure very well. Martin was nice, though, and was happy to have Jordan working for him so long as she was sober.

Milo had been hired there too. When Colby had told him she was done with stealing, he'd told Gram that he was done too. Gram bristled but didn't try to talk him out of it. And then he'd decided that his baby's father wasn't going to be having sex for money either, so he got a job at the Velo too, even though the money was tragically little compared to what he used to make.

But it was a job. And it had nothing to do with drugs or sex, which Colby was thrilled about. She hated that he used to have sex with skanky old men. It was probably pure luck that he hadn't caught some nasty disease. Luck—and condoms. Which he was usually very serious about. Except for that one time.

Milo might have looked harder for a better job, but he liked Jordan, and he liked Martin, and he really liked the tall, lanky barista called Etienne. Etienne wore jeans folded up to his calves, and pale blue canvas shoes, and short-sleeved button-up shirts with bowties. And a hint of eyeliner, which actually looked really good on him and made his green eyes sparkle.

The day that Colby went into labor, she hadn't had any practice contractions for ages. Labor wasn't even on her mind, other than the constant reminder of her enormous belly.

There she was, sitting in the café with Milo, who had just finished his shift. Jordan and Etienne were working.

Colby had reached for her iced mocha, about to scoop a finger of whipped cream into her mouth, when all of a sudden she felt a warm, spreading wetness between her legs.

"Oh, no," she whispered. "No, I didn't."

"Didn't what?" Milo said, not really interested. He was looking at ads for apartments. He had to move out of his studio. He'd finally admitted to Colby that it had been subsidized by a guy who ran several gay bars in the West End. He'd let Milo stay there for cheap in exchange for regular favors.

"My water just broke."

"Your water just—" Milo realized exactly what Colby was saying.

He leaped up. "Your water just broke!"
He spun around and yelled, "Her water
just broke! We're having a BABY!"
He jumped up and down, literally
squealing. "Oh my god. OH MY GOD!
Let's go! We have to get your hospital
bag. It's at Gram's, right?"

Colby nodded.

"Okay, okay."

Jordan tore off her apron and ran
to Colby's side. "What do you need?
Name it. It's yours. I'm here. Totally
here for you."

Colby put up her hands. "Everybody
slow down. The baby is not coming
right this minute." All of a sudden Colby
was gripped by an intense pain. She
held her breath until it passed. "At least,
I hope not."

"We have to go!" Milo shouted.

"My pants are wet."

"Come with me." Jordan helped her
to the staff room and gave her a pair of

her pants. "Bonus of being fat is that these will fit you."

The first cabbie who stopped drove off when he saw Colby buckle with pain during a contraction. The second agreed to take them as far as Gram's but wouldn't wait to take them on to the hospital.

"Asshole," Jordan said when she'd paid the driver.

"We'll get Gram's car," Milo said.

The three of them went inside. Milo put a towel down on the couch and instructed Colby to sit there. But she didn't want to sit. She wanted to walk. She paced the room, talking to the midwife on the phone, telling her what was happening.

Jordan found the hospital bag.

Gram came running. "I'll drive!" She grabbed her purse.

"Where's Gigi?" Colby asked when she hung up the phone.

"I don't know," Gram said, steering everyone to the door. "She didn't come home last night. Maybe with that boy."

"He's no boy, Gram." Colby winced as another wave of pain hit her. Gigi was dating a drug dealer who was at least twice her age. "Arman is a creepy MAN. He's no good."

"Well, no good or not"—Gram grabbed Colby's arm and pulled her up—"he's not here. She's not here. And you are having my great-grand-baby. Let's go." She'd long given up her ungay-Milo hopes, but she was ecstatic about the baby being a blood relation, accident or not.

By the time Colby got into a birthing room, her contractions were coming fast and strong. She wanted to walk, though, and growled at Milo when he suggested she get onto the bed. She didn't want to lie down. Not at all. She wanted to pace.

Jordan, wisely, said nothing. She had a couple of tennis balls and was massaging Colby's lower back with them the way the midwife had shown her. Colby rested her head on her arms and leaned against the wall, moaning.

"No lesbian jokes," Colby muttered between contractions.

"Nope."

"Just keep doing that though."

"You like it like this?" Jordan said with a smile in her voice.

"I said no lesbian jokes."

"No lesbian jokes."

Colby only asked for drugs one time, and that was when she was already pushing and it felt like she was trying to pass a semi-truck, but then she delivered the baby's head and everything got a lot easier.

Not painless, no. But easier than straight-up contractions.

The baby slipped out, and everyone in the room cheered as the midwife wiped the baby's face and placed the squalling, tiny thing on Colby's chest.

Colby cried and cried—and then thought to look at the baby.

A girl. A *daughter*.

She had a daughter.

She was a mom.

This was her kid.

"A girl," she whispered.

Milo leaned over. "A little girl."

"Wow," Jordan said.

"Thank God." Gram kissed her cross necklace. "A healthy baby girl."

And she *was* healthy. Colby was moved to a private room with a chair that unfolded into a bed for the dad. But Milo was getting antsy and didn't want to stay, so Jordan was the one who ended up sleeping on the fold-out cot. The nurses came in several times during the night to check on Colby and the baby, who was supposed to sleep in a plastic bucket beside the bed.

"A bassinet," the nurse said.

"A plastic bucket." Colby kept the baby with her instead, against her chest and against the nurse's orders.

"You're young," the nurse admonished her when she came in and found Colby still cuddling the baby to her. "You don't know any better."

"This is *my* baby," Colby said. "I know best."

"You're what, seventeen?" The nurse glanced at Colby's chart.

Jordan, who'd been only half-asleep, stood up. "How old are you?"

"None of your business," said the nurse.

"Neither is the fact that she doesn't want her baby to sleep in a plastic bucket after spending nine months all nice and cozy inside."

"I'm calling the social worker," the nurse said. She pointed a finger at Colby. "I know your history, kid."

It was probably Mr. Horvath who came by first thing the next morning. But Colby was already gone. She'd wrapped the baby up in the blanket Gram had knit, and with Jordan's help, they took the bus home. To Gram's.

Gigi in the night

Colby named her baby Luna Grace. *Luna* for the big moon she spent so many hours gazing at from her window at Meadow Farm. *Grace* for her mom.

Milo wanted to name her Scarlet Ruby, but Colby vetoed that as super dumb. Jordan figured they should name her something more gender neutral, like Taylor or Kelly. Or Jordan.

Gram loved the name, just as she loved everything about the baby. Colby could've named her Dump Truck Sani-Station and Gram would've sung it in a lullaby without so much as blinking.

And Gigi?

Well, she hadn't met her niece yet.

Luna was a week old, and Gigi hadn't even seen her. She'd come once to get clothes and look for a mascara, but Colby had only just fallen asleep with Luna after a really long, hard night and Gram forbade Gigi to even tiptoe into the room. Not even to look for the missing mascara.

When Colby woke up later, she cried. "I would've wanted her to meet Luna, Gram."

"You needed sleep." Gram put a plate in front of Colby. Peanut butter on toast. A mug of hot, milky tea. "Besides, she was in no state to meet a new little baby." She shook her head and made a disapproving *tut-tut* sound.

Gigi didn't meet Luna until she was almost three weeks old, and even then, it was hardly a proper introduction. If Gigi needed anything, she came by in the middle of the night. Even if Colby was awake, she'd pretend not to be. It was awkward now. There was too much space between them. They were so far apart now, Colby wasn't sure how she'd ever get back to Gigi. Or get Gigi to come back to her.

One night when Gigi came into the room, Colby was wide awake. Luna was asleep beside her, tucked in one of those Baby-Safe Sleeper thingies. Colby had just nursed her and was almost asleep too, but not quite.

Colby shut her eyes when she heard Gigi come in. And she would've stayed like that, pretending to be asleep, except that she heard Gigi rooting under Colby's bed.

The jewelry box.

Colby turned over. "Hey."

Gigi raised her phone, the light on it making Colby squint. "Hey."

"What are you doing?" Colby sat up. She turned on the bedside lamp.

"Nothing."

Gigi had the jewelry box in her hands.

"That's mine."

"Hell no, it's not."

Colby reached for the box. Gigi backed up into the small circle of light. She was gaunt. Scratches lined one cheek. Her eyes darted back and forth, back and forth, dark shadows underneath them.

"I watch her, you know." Gigi coughed. She reached for Colby's water glass beside the bed and took a drink. "When I come at night. I watch her sleeping. She looks like you. Milo too. Her nose. His nose. My nose. The family nose."

"I haven't seen you watching her."

"I know you pretend to be asleep." Gigi laughed. "But sometimes you actually are asleep."

"Put the box down." Colby still had every intention of returning it. She just hadn't had a chance yet.

Much to her surprise, Gigi set the box beside Colby on the bed.

"Thank you." Colby took it and held it in her lap.

Then she knew. All of a sudden she knew.

She opened the box.

It was empty except for the earrings and the child's bracelet.

"Gigi?" Colby looked up at her. Her voice knotted in her throat. "Where's the rest of it?"

"I took it." Gigi shrugged. "Why not? It wasn't doing anyone any good hiding under your bed. Gram takes care of you. You get welfare. I need money. You don't."

"Oh, Gigi…"

Gigi lurched forward to get a better look at Luna.

"It doesn't make any sense." Gigi gazed at the baby. "You and Milo. And Jordan. That baby."

"It makes sense."

"Not really."

"It's like you stayed back, Gigi. Behind us," Colby said. "In the past."

"It's like you took off and went somewhere else entirely, Colby." Gigi pulled a backpack off her shoulder and set it on the floor, rummaging through it in that frenetic way junkies do that makes everything seem so much harder than it needs to be. "I got this for her." She pulled out a soft, pink blanket with satin edging and *Luna Grace* embroidered along the bottom. "From that place in the mall where we got those matching shirts done last year. For Christmas."

"Ho."

"Ho."

Colby laughed. "And when we stood side by side—"

"Ho, ho," Gigi said. And then, "Give me the box."

"No." Colby tightened her grip on it. "I want to give it back."

"What's the point now? There's hardly anything left."

"There's a point. Even if you can't see it."

"I need the money, Cole."

"You need help."

"Oh, right. Well, thanks for letting me know."

"You need rehab, Gigi."

"No thanks."

"Why not?"

"Why should I?"

"Because you're a drug addict."

"Preach it, sister."

"You won't go because of Arman, right?" Her drug-dealer boyfriend.

"Leave him out of it." Gigi glowered at Colby. "Give me the box."

"No."

"Fine." Gigi lunged for it, trying to wrestle it out of Colby's hands. Colby held tight, and Gigi gave her a shove.

"Stop it!" Colby shoved back, still holding tight to the box. "Careful of the baby!"

Then Luna began to cry.

Colby let go of the box at once. She turned to her baby and scooped her up into her arms.

Gigi stuffed the jewelry box into her backpack. "You don't see what's happening, but I do."

"You have no clue, Gigi."

"I know exactly what's happening." She nearly spat the words. "You've taken everything that was ever mine.

My room, my house, my gram, even my brother! I hate you, Colby. I really do."

Colby sat on the edge of the bed. Tears rolled down her cheeks. She held her baby and stared at her, willing herself not to say anything. To just let Gigi go. Gigi hadn't hit rock bottom yet. Colby wondered if she ever would. When they used to get high together, they watched out for each other. But now Gigi was alone out there.

"I love you, Gigi. No matter what, I love you."

But Gigi was gone.

When Luna stopped crying, Colby could hear Gigi arguing with Gram by the front door. But Gram couldn't stop Gigi either. She slammed the door behind her, and then the tiny house rang with simple, painful silence.

playing house

Jordan and Milo were looking for a place together. At first Colby wanted to move in with them too, but every place they looked at said no babies. So Colby put her name in for social housing and settled in to wait, no matter how badly she wanted to get away from the neighborhood.

Milo and Jordan had saved just enough for a deposit and first month's rent.

They'd intended to wait a bit longer, to save up more money, but they were looking for a place now because the club owner had moved a new boy toy into the studio and Milo was sleeping on the couch at Gram's.

"Not saying that I won't miss the loft," Milo said more than once. "But I don't miss the sweat and aftershave. Ugh."

Colby was going with them to see a one-bedroom apartment above a convenience store down the block from the Velo Café.

So far, it hadn't mattered if Jordan and Milo had the money and good references. Every landlord had rejected their application. They were too young. Too weird.

This one was different though.

Jordan and Milo's boss, Martin, knew the landlord, who also owned the convenience store. He'd put in a good word for them.

Gurdeep met them at the store.

"I'll show you. Nice place. You can have it if you want. Martin says you will take good care of it." Then he narrowed his eyes and leaned in. "No funny business though. No drugs in my building. None. I see drugs, I smell drugs—I know drugs. No drugs in here. Am I clear?"

"Yes, sir," Jordan said.

"Totally clear," Milo said.

"And who are you?" Gurdeep cast a glance at Colby, who held Luna in her arms.

"I—uh, I'm a friend."

"Not you." Gurdeep's face brightened. He grinned. "That baby. Who is that cute little bundle?"

"Oh." Colby moved Luna's hood back so he could see her. "This is Luna."

"I like babies." Gurdeep pulled a fat collection of keys from his pocket. "Babies make life much happier. I have four babies. They are all grown now.

Not so cute. Thank God for grand-children. Come on. Let me show you the apartment."

Milo and Jordan and Colby grinned at each other, then followed Gurdeep out of the store, through a door beside it and up two flights of stairs.

The hallway was musty, and the walls were filthy.

There were two doors on each side and a window at the end, overlooking the street.

"Martin said you want one bedroom." Gurdeep sorted through his keys. "But I think two bedrooms better for you. More room for the baby."

Colby brightened. "You'd let us? With the baby too?"

"Sure." Gurdeep smiled. "Why not?"

"Do you have a two-bedroom?"

"I do. This one." Gurdeep led them to the last door on the right. He unlocked it and swung it open. "More expensive.

But more space. I don't mind babies. Many landlords will not rent to babies. But I have nine grandchildren, and I know babies are not the trouble. Druggies are the trouble. Always the druggies. You promise me you not do any drugs in here—no drugs ever—and I am happy to have your baby as one of my valued tenants."

Colby's mind was spinning.

The apartment was warm. She could hear the traffic swishing along the wet streets below. Rain pattering on the eaves under the window.

The ceilings were high, the windows too. Not as high as Milo's old place, but tall enough to make the place feel bigger than it was. Both big windows overlooked the street. Colby stood at the first window. From there she could see the park, with its new playground and community garden.

A narrow, rare stretch of open sky above the buildings. Perfect for looking at the moon.

She didn't care what the rest of the place looked like. She wanted to live there.

"This would be my room." Milo emerged from a doorway. "And I'm not sharing."

"Check out this pantry." Jordan gestured to a skinny door off the tiny kitchen.

Pantry or closet, Colby wasn't sure. No window. But fairly big. For a closet.

The other bedroom was beside the pantry, overlooking the street. "This would be your room, Jordan." But already, Colby was imagining it as hers.

"I'll sleep in that pantry thing," Jordan said. "You have this one."

"No!"

"I like it cozy. I can fit a double bed in there. Hang some lights. Make it into my love palace." Jordan laughed at herself. She'd only had one proper girlfriend. Before Meadow Farm. And that hadn't lasted long.

"I can't take the bedroom, Jordan. This was supposed to be your and Milo's place."

"I'm giving you the bedroom. It's the chivalrous thing to do. Besides, you and Luna need the room. I just need a bed. Hell, a single would do."

"Not forever."

"Let me do this for you." Jordan put her arm around Colby. Luna mewled, her eyes opening. "Let me do this for you. And Luna Grace. You know that I want to, right? And I won't take no for an answer. Seriously, Colby. I'm offering to go into the *closet* for you. If only so that I can make jokes about coming out of the closet every morning."

Gram cried when she drove Colby and Luna and their trunkload of things to the new place. But when she saw the tidy little apartment, and the room that would be Colby and Luna's, she kissed Colby on both cheeks and told her that she could come home anytime, especially for dinner.

Gram didn't mention Gigi, and Colby didn't ask. Colby hadn't spoken to her since they'd argued about the jewelry box. She knew that Gigi was coming and going from Gram's place though. Food gone missing. Her clothes piled atop the washing machine, waiting for Gram to take pity on them. Makeup strewn in the bathroom. Wet towels on the floor.

Colby held on to these little signs of life, pocketing them like so many morsels of hope. Gigi was still there. In the shadows, maybe. But not gone.

the fox and the moon

If Colby didn't think about Gigi or her dad, she could almost pretend that nothing was wrong. She had a home and people who loved her and a little baby who was her entire world. She was content. Maybe for the first time in her life. Or since her mom died, anyway. Sometimes Colby fantasized that her life was a lot like this before her mom died.

Peaceful and busy. Filled with life and people and joy.

Colby was thinking about this one morning when there was a knock at the door.

It was her social worker, Mr. Horvath.

"Hey." And even though she'd dodged him since Luna's birth, she opened the door wide. She had nothing to hide. "Come on in."

Mr. Horvath hesitated, one hand on the doorjamb. "Not the reaction I expected from the girl who disappeared."

"Sorry."

He shook his head. "Why'd you give me a fake address?"

"Well, you found me now."

"I had to track you down through Jordan's mom. Not impressed by your disappearing act, Colby."

"In the flesh, standing in front of you. Asking you in." Colby stepped back, bowing slightly. "Come in. Please."

"This is where you're living?"

"Yes."

"Your name is on the lease?"

"Yes."

Mr. Horvath was still frowning. Colby started to get nervous. He had the power to take Luna. What if he didn't believe that everything was as awesome as it seemed?

"You were doing so well there for a while, Colby." Mr. Horvath shook his head.

"I'm still doing great." Colby's voice rose. "Me and Luna are doing great."

"The urine tests and parenting classes and twelve-step meetings are not optional, Colby."

"Look, test my piss, if you want. I'm clean." It came out angrier than Colby intended, but she was really scared now. "I'm sorry, Mr. Horvath. I just…I just, I don't know. I just hate that shit. I don't want to be the ex-junkie mama.

I just want to be a regular mama, you know?"

"But you're not. You are an ex-junkie."

"I know, but—"

"But nothing, Colby." Mr. Horvath put a hand on her shoulder. "Most teen mothers in your situation don't leave the hospital with their babies. And the stunt you pulled, leaving early?" He shook his head. "The nurse wanted me to apprehend Luna immediately. I assured her that you'd been clean for a long time. I hope I was right."

"I *was* clean. I *am* clean. I've been clean since Meadow Farm."

"Which is why you have your daughter with you now. And you were doing really well, coming in regularly. Going to meetings."

"I'm sorry, Mr. Horvath." Colby heard a catch in her voice. "With the move, I just...I'm not sure. I'm sorry."

"Well. Apology accepted." He stepped into the apartment, his eyes doing a fast sweep before Colby could hide anything. "Who else lives here?"

"My baby's father, Milo. And Jordan. They both bat for your team." Colby tried a smile.

Mr. Horvath stared at her. "And how is that relevant?"

But then a different look came across his face. He looked confused. "Wait a minute. Milo's the baby's father? Isn't he—"

"Gay."

"How—" Mr. Horvath caught himself. "No. None of my business. Rude to ask. Sorry."

"I was hoping that he'd jump the fence."

As if he'd heard them talking, Milo opened his bedroom door and stumbled out.

"Who's he?" Milo yawned.

"My social worker."

"And what do you want?" Milo crossed his arms, suddenly defensive. "We've got everything Luna needs. Even two parents. Hell, three, if you want to count Jordan, who is about as good with babies as someone can be. How many of your teenage moms can say that the dad is in the picture, huh? How many? And you know what? None of us are using drugs. We even smoke outside. Look around! You won't even find an ashtray. So? What are you doing here?"

Mr. Horvath held out his hand, "And you're the—"

"Gay baby daddy." They shook hands.

"Mr. Horvath. Nice to meet you.

"So, *you're* the fantastic Mr. Fox." Milo grinned. "Let me give you a tour of our very baby-friendly little abode.

I think you'll like Colby and Luna's room the best."

Colby trailed behind them as Milo upsold the apartment as if it were something out of an interior-decorating magazine. And while Milo had done a nice job of kicking some life and color into the few drab pieces of furniture they'd got from Gram's, it was still just a dingy East Vancouver rental.

Then he opened the door to Colby and Luna's room.

Jordan and Milo had gone all out for this room. One end had a little sitting area, with a comfy chair for nursing and a little area rug and a big, glowing orb of a hanging lamp with fairy lights strung from it as if it were the full moon in the night sky, keeping watch.

Milo had covered the old chair with soft purple fabric. He'd found material for curtains with the same purple in it and tiny silver stars. It was Colby's favorite place in the apartment, followed shortly by Luna's corner of the room.

"Foxes," Mr. Horvath said quietly.

"There's yours." The little plastic fox sat on the windowsill above the crib, keeping watch. "The first one." Colby pointed to two stuffed foxes perched on the change table. "See? No stuffies in the crib. We read about that. And no crib bumpers either. Not safe."

Milo had photocopied images of foxes from children's books and framed them in mismatched thrift-store frames that he'd painted pale purple.

"You still need to do random urine tests, Colby. And the parenting classes. And the meetings." He picked up the fox that Colby had stolen from him so long ago. "And we need to talk. Make a plan for you and Luna. Everything seems perfect here. It does. But I know that perfect is pretty hard to maintain, especially as an ex-junkie."

"I'm not an ex-junkie." Colby felt a tightening in her chest. "I'm a recovering addict."

"You going to NA meetings?"

"No."

"Then you're still an ex-junkie."

"I went to rehab!" Colby nearly shouted. "I told you, I'm clean. It's not fair to keep calling me a junkie."

The door to the pantry creaked open and Jordan popped her head out.

"Everything okay?"

"No. My social worker thinks I'm still a junkie."

"*Ex*-junkie," Mr. Horvath said. "You can't do it by yourself, Colby. And it's part of your parental agreement, if you remember the papers you signed when you got back from rehab, when you decided to keep your baby? Urine tests. Twelve-step meetings. The Nobody's

Perfect Parenting Program that you haven't signed up for."

"I know. I just couldn't do it."

"Not an option," Mr. Horvath said. "It's a condition of you having custody of your child."

"What?" Milo turned to Colby. "You were supposed to be doing stuff? I didn't know." He spoke to Mr. Horvath now. "If I had, I would've made sure she did all that. I'm sorry, Mr. Fox. We'll get on it. Immediately."

"Mr. Fox? I'll admit, that's cute." Mr. Horvath set the fox back where he'd found it, which helped ease the panic in Colby's throat. "And I appreciate your sentiment, Milo. I do. But Colby is the one who has to do the things expected of her. You can do the parenting program too. And the twelve-step meetings. That'd be awesome—"

"I will. Totally will."

"—but I need Colby to do it too. Willingly."

Luna yawned in Colby's arms, stretching her tiny fists into the air.

Colby smiled down at her. She put her finger to Luna's cheek. "I meant to. I guess I've just been—"

"Super busy," Milo cut in. "There's a lot to looking after a new baby."

"Yeah," Colby said. "And I'm in love. Totally and completely in love. With Luna Grace. At first it was just full-on baby, you know? And then, once we moved out of Gram's place, it felt like a new start. And I didn't want to bring any of the old stuff along. I can't even imagine going to some stupid twelve-step meeting. It's like it'd make everything dirty. When it's so nice and clean, you know?"

"Well, see that you do get out the door to stupid twelve-step meetings. And the

parenting classes. And for the pee tests."
Mr. Horvath made for the front door.
"You're not the first recovering-addict/
ex-junkie teenage mom I've had dealings
with." His tone softened as he continued.
"But I will say that I have a lot of hope
for you, Colby. You have a really good
thing going here."

steps

The parenting program was lame. Colby
had an incredibly strong gut instinct
when it came to Luna. Starting with
leaving the hospital early and ever since,
she was positive that she knew best.
She liked to think that it was because
her own mom had been the same way,
but Colby couldn't know. She couldn't
ask her dad. And there was no one else.

The other girls in the program—there were a few dads, too, but they mostly sat silent, slouched in their chairs, looking bored—seemed so nervous about their babies.

Not Colby. She knew exactly how she wanted to do things. Take feeding, for example. Colby was the only one who nursed. And she planned to for as long as she could. That's what her boobs were for, after all. All the other girls gave their babies bottles. And they left them lying in their strollers for hours and hours at a time, crying, while they texted on their phones and smoked and were generally nasty skanks.

Nobody's Perfect was entertaining enough, she supposed. Milo came with her, and he camped it up to the point where the other guys hated him and his Super Gay Daddy act. But he made Colby laugh.

The twelve-step meetings were pretty good though.

She could admit that.

Held at the Legion by the SkyTrain station, it was full of freaky East Van folks. Jordan and Milo came with her, and Luna too, usually asleep in Colby's arms.

At first they sat at the very back, in the last three chairs on the right. They spent the whole meeting whispering and laughing about what everybody was wearing. Or saying. Or doing. Or the color of their hair. Or what they had pierced.

But then one day a woman met them at the door. She was tiny and skinny, with short-cropped hair and a full sleeve of tattoos down each arm, of trees and crows and sky. She looked tough, but her smile was welcoming enough.

"Hey. I've noticed you guys. Acting like brats at the back of the meeting." She blocked their way. "You're not going to do that today, right?"

"We didn't—" Milo started to protest.

"You did."

"We weren't actually being—" Jordan started.

"Mean?" The woman cocked her head to one side. "Yes, you were. What low-life assholes come to an NA meeting to tear people down? A room full of people trying to get clean or stay clean. Really. That's super low."

"We're really sorry," Colby said. "We thought no one could hear us."

"And that makes it any better?" She glanced at Luna. "What are you teaching your kid by being so mean?"

"Hey, now." Jordan bristled. "Leave Luna out of it."

"But she's part of it, right?" The woman held out her hand. "Shauna. And you are?"

"Jordan." Jordan put a protective arm around Colby. "This is Colby. And that's Milo."

"And Luna." Shauna put a finger on Luna's arm. She cooed at her, which surprised Colby. "My youngest is almost one." She looked up at Colby. "You need hand-me-downs?"

"I...uh..." Colby wasn't sure what to say. She'd just been scolded by the very same woman who was now offering her hand-me-downs for Luna? "Yes. We could use some more sleepers, for sure."

"Honey, I have a garbage bag full of really cute stuff. My sister buys gorgeous things. You'll love them. Not all pink either."

Colby laughed, still nervous. She knew the scolding part wasn't done. She waited, unsure what to do next.

"This is the deal." Shauna stepped away from the door. "You're welcome in, but not if you guys pull that shit at the back. Tonight you sit at the front. With me."

bracelet

That's how Shauna came to be Colby's sponsor.

And reliable source of excellent hand-me-downs, the best being a sling that Colby could tuck Luna into and have her arms free. She used it all the time, and it made doing things so much easier. Instead of dragging the stroller onto the crowded bus, or being passed by the bus because it already had its limit of strollers and walkers and wheelchairs, Colby could get on any bus with Luna snugged into the sling.

Colby was on the bus heading to her appointment with Mr. Fox, which was how she thought of Mr. Horvath now. He didn't mind the nickname, and most times he gave Colby one of his toy foxes to add to Luna's collection.

That day, Colby had one for him. As a thank-you for everything. It was an antique playing card with two foxes on the back. She'd bought a frame for it at the dollar store and set the card against a piece of dark brown paper, so that the orange of the foxes really stood out.

She was very pleased with it and was holding it in her lap, admiring it, while Luna slept in the sling.

"What's with the foxes?"

Gigi.

At first, Colby didn't know what to say. She was taken aback by Gigi's appearance.

She was gaunt, with dark shadows under her eyes and sores all over one side of her face and down one arm.

"Gigi?" Colby whispered her name. She reached out and took her hand, gingerly, guiding her into the empty seat beside her. "Are you okay?"

"Yeah." Gigi leaned her head against Colby's shoulder and closed her eyes. "No. It doesn't matter."

Luna looked at the stranger beside them. She giggled. She could almost sit up by herself now. She reached out a hand, but Gigi didn't see.

"Where've you been?"

"Around." Gigi roused. She dug in her purse. "I have something for you."

"Nothing sketchy, right, Gigi?" Colby checked to see who was watching them. "Don't ask me to hold anything for you. Nothing to do with drugs. I'm clean now. I don't want to mess it up."

"I get it." Disappointment flashed across Gigi's face. She pulled out a tiny square of folded paper. "I get it, Cole."

"Sorry." Colby wished she hadn't said anything about drugs. "It's just... I get tested. Like, that's where I'm headed right now. I don't want them anywhere near me or Luna."

"I said, I get it." Gigi stood up. "Here." She pressed the piece of paper into Colby's hand. Before Colby could look at it, Gigi dug in her purse again. She pulled out the child's bracelet from the jewelry box. The jewelry box they'd fought over. She held it out, dangling it on one finger. "Here. For your baby."

"For your *niece*."

"This is my stop." Gigi let the bracelet drop into Colby's lap.

"Where are you going?" As she stood up, Colby grabbed Gigi's thin wrist. "Come with me. My social worker is great. I can get you into rehab. Come on, Gigi. Stop living like this."

"I like my life, okay?" Gigi pulled away and wobbled toward the back door. The bus stopped. The door didn't open though. Gigi pounded halfheartedly on the glass. "Back door! Open the back door!"

The driver opened the door, and Gigi stumbled out. Colby pressed her face to the window and mouthed, *I love you*.

Gigi stood there for a moment, almost glowing with decay against the dirty gray concrete, and then she made the *I love you* sign back.

Everything

"I don't know about this," Jordan said. Colby, Milo and Jordan were about a block away from the house.

In Colby's pocket was the bracelet. The only thing left from their haul. Colby was going to give it back.

"Why don't we just mail it?" Milo said.

"We're not going to tell them we did it," Colby explained again. "We'll say it was our friend, who felt bad—which we do—and wanted to give back the bracelet."

"We could say it was Gigi," Jordan offered.

"No!" Milo and Colby both barked.

There was the house.

And this time, there were people home.

Splashing and happy kid screams came from the backyard. Colby remembered seeing the pool, but it had been covered when they were there before. There were two kids in the family, according to Gigi's information. Colby wondered which one the bracelet belonged to.

"I'll do it by myself," she said, striding up the front steps.

So Jordan and Milo hung back at the bottom of the steps, practically cowering.

Colby rang the doorbell.

Long, torturous minutes passed.

A woman wearing a uniform opened the door.

"May I help you?"

Colby glanced at Jordan and Milo, who nodded. But Colby didn't want to give it to the housekeeper.

"Can I speak to the lady of the house?" she asked. The words sounded strange. Archaic.

"And you are?"

"I, uh…" All of a sudden Colby wasn't sure about this at all. When she and Shauna were talking about amends, Colby had thought giving the bracelet back was a great idea, but now it seemed stupid and dangerous. Still… she wanted to do it. "I have something of hers that I'd like to return."

The woman frowned at her. "Wait here."

She closed the door.

Colby spun around, one hand on Luna in the sling, the other held out, imploring her friends for help.

Jordan and Milo shook their heads and stood a little closer together.

"Thanks." Colby turned her back to them. "Thanks a lot."

Luna reached up and patted Colby's chest. "Thanks, Luna. Good to know someone cares."

The door opened again, and a slender woman stood in front of her, wearing a cotton dress over a swimsuit, damp hair pulled back into a sleek ponytail.

"What can I do for you?"

"This is yours." Colby held out the bracelet. "Right?"

The woman went pale. She took the bracelet, staring at it in the palm of her hand for a moment and then suddenly sliding to the floor and sitting in a folded heap of dress and legs.

"Where did you get this?" she whispered.

Colby hadn't expected this reaction. Surprise or anger, even relief. But not this. And Colby wasn't even sure what it was.

"Where did you get this?" the woman asked, looking up. There were tears in her eyes. In that moment, she seemed to collect herself. Almost as if an unseen hand was lifting her up and putting her back together. It was like watching a puzzle picture take shape. She asked again, much more sharply. "Where did you get this? Answer me."

"A friend gave it to me to give to you," Colby said.

"A friend?" The woman shook her head. "This same 'friend' who robbed us? Is that right?"

"I don't know." Colby backed down the stairs. "But she said to give it back to you."

"This bracelet belongs—*belonged*—to my daughter." The tears started again. "She was three when she got cancer. We buried her eleven days after her fourth birthday. She never took it off. *I* took it off. Of her dead body. Do you understand? I took this bracelet off my child's *dead body.*"

The housekeeper appeared beside the woman. "Come, Mrs. Ellis. Come now."

"Off her dead body," the woman repeated. Her shoulders slacked, and a tiny smile formed on her lips. "But I—"

"I'm sorry," Colby said. She held Luna tightly. Her own tears threatened to spill. "I'm so sorry."

"Let's go," Milo called.

"Come on!" Jordan said.

They were clearly anxious about what was going on. About what Colby might say next. What she might admit to.

Colby wasn't thinking about the robbery though.

She was thinking about the woman's child.

She was thinking about her own baby.

She was thinking about her own mother.

She was thinking about everything that had ever gone wrong.

She was thinking about Gigi.

About how the thing that had held the least value for Gigi was so valuable to this woman. How taking something had caused so much pain. How awful it was that Colby had made it worse. How they'd all made it worse.

Colby wanted to tell Gigi how good it was that she'd given the bracelet back. How holding on to the bracelet had made such a big difference. How she'd done a small, shining good thing amid all the gloom.

"Let's close the door now." The housekeeper started to pushed the door shut, but the woman stopped her.

"Thank you," she said. "For bringing it back."

And then she slammed the door in Colby's face, the noise of it ringing in her ears.

grandpa

Before she had Luna, Colby would've never simply forgotten the little piece of paper that Gigi had given her. But looking after Luna was pretty much all-consuming, and so sometimes things fell away. Details. Specifics. Un-baby stuff. Like the tiny folded square of paper.

And then Gigi died.

Dead from a heroin overdose, slumped in a piss-stink doorway in the alley behind the Carnegie Community Centre. A month after her eighteenth birthday.

The staff at the Carnegie said she had come for the two-dollar supper, already high. She had used the bathroom. Made a call on the free phone at the front desk. Got some condoms and tampons from the health nurse. The security guard at the back door said she left with her boyfriend. He described an older guy. Arman.

But the camera at the back corner showed her shuffling down the alley behind Hastings Street alone. She turned at the last minute, lifting her hand to push her hair off her shoulders. She lifted her chin just a tiny bit.

The security guard emailed Colby the clip. A gray, blurry treasure.

Colby played the short clip over and over and over and over.

In that moment, Colby could see a glimpse of the real Gigi. The one who would've blown the camera a kiss. The Gigi who would never have left without saying goodbye. The Gigi who was supposed to be Luna's auntie.

The Gigi who had kept sliding into the dark, until nothing was left but heavy, permanent night, with not a star to be seen.

That's when Colby remembered the tiny piece of paper. With a surge of hope, she emptied out her diaper bag. Maybe it was a note from Gigi. Maybe whatever was on the paper would explain something. Anything. Even just a tiny piece of it.

But she couldn't find it.

She slid her hand down each pocket, felt every seam in every crevice.

Luna sat on the floor beside her, gnawing on a forgotten rubber fox from the dumped-out pile.

Colby was done with crying. She was mad now. Mad at herself for not doing more to help Gigi, and mad at Gigi for dying.

The paper. There it was, stuck in the bottom mesh-sided pocket, brown and sticky from spilled coffee.

Colby pulled it out, heart pounding. It was tiny, about the size of a ketchup packet folded in half. The edges were worn, and as she unfolded it, it fell into four pieces.

A puzzle. Colby laughed, carefully placing the pieces in order. Like Gigi.

But it wasn't from Gigi.

It was her dad's spindly writing, tiny and hard to read.

Colby—I'm at the Balmoral. Room 28. Would love to see you. Sorry for everything. Gigi says you have a baby.

I'd like to meet her. And see you. Love, your no-good, screw-up, junkie Dad. p.s. 42 days clean!!!

Colby sighed. She smiled at Luna. "Your auntie Gigi could've told me that she'd seen him." There was no date on the note. No idea when he wrote it. Or if he was still at the Balmoral. Or still clean.

Colby pulled the baby into her lap and kissed the top of her head. "Your grandpa wants to meet you. That sounds weird."

Colby got on a bus right away and headed downtown. Her old neighborhood. Past Gram's pawnshop. Colby peered in as the bus passed. Gram was sitting in the easy chair beside the front door. She looked older now. As if Gigi's death had chopped years off her own life.

The Balmoral.

Room 28.

The door was sticky with cockroach poo. Someone at the end of the hall yelled behind a closed door. The forced happiness of a laugh track on someone's TV blared from the next door.

Colby knocked.

She heard shuffling. Then the lock. For a brief moment, Colby considered leaving. Right now. Before he saw her. So much time had passed. So much had happened. And if he wasn't clean, she didn't want him near Luna.

The door opened.

"Dad?"

"Colby." He pulled her into a hug. In that moment, Colby knew she'd never let him go again. No matter what.

The day of the funeral, Colby's dad held his granddaughter as if she were either going to barf on him or break into a million pieces.

"You have to hold her like you mean it, Dad." Colby lifted Luna from his arms and demonstrated. "She likes to know that whoever is holding her isn't going to drop her."

Colby passed Luna back to him. He held her more like a sack of sugar now.

"That's better."

The funeral home was four blocks from Gram's shop. Everybody else was already there. The service was going to start in twenty minutes. Colby's dad walked slowly. He'd had a bad fall around the time that Luna was born, and he limped now. He looked ten years older than he was, except when he smiled. He still had a dimple when he smiled. Colby had the same one. Luna too.

Jordan and Milo met them outside.

"Not many people in there," Milo said. "There should be more. Mom is wailing, as if she has the right to."

Gigi and Milo's mother had been granted a day pass from prison.

"She's Gigi's *mom*."

"Hardly." Milo laughed. He'd grown harder since Gigi's death. Angrier. "Gram was more of a mom to Gigi than she ever was. It's our mom's fault that Gigi ended up a junkie in the first place."

"Still," Colby said softly.

The chapel was empty except for two rows at the front. Gram sat beside her daughter. There was a handful of regular customers from the pawnshop. A small, jittery clutch of Gigi's street friends at one end of the second row. Shauna, alongside Milo's sponsor, Ben. Mr. Fox. No Arman.

Colby sat with her dad on one side of her and Shauna on the other. Mr. Fox reached across Shauna and handed Colby a tiny porcelain fox, no bigger than a Monopoly game piece. A tiny heart was painted on its white chest. It was a hopeful thing that she could hold tight in the palm of her hand, but still, it made Colby incredibly, deeply sad.

That night Colby placed the new fox alongside the others. It was the smallest one. The most fragile. The only one with its heart on the outside.

Colby sat rocking Luna to sleep beside the open window. A warm summer breeze drifted in. Traffic noises from the street below. Shouts of joy from the café on the corner, where they were watching European soccer. Two little kids arguing over a toy truck. Dogs barking in the park.

Colby looked up. The moon was full, passing in and out of sight as clouds shifted across the city skyline. The world was quieter now with Gigi gone.